Walt Disney's
Snow White
and the Seven Dwarfs

THE SCARIEST ONE OF ALL

by Irene Trimble ❖ illustrated by Atelier Philippe Harchy

Random House 🏠 New York

A Random House PICTUREBACK® Shape Book

Copyright © 2002 Disney Enterprises, Inc. All rights reserved under International and Pan-American Copyright Conventions.
Published in the United States by Random House, Inc., New York,
and simultaneously in Canada by Random House of Canada Limited, Toronto, in conjunction with Disney Enterprises, Inc.
PICTUREBACK, RANDOM HOUSE, and the Random House colophon are registered trademarks of Random House, Inc.
Library of Congress Control Number: 20001091906
ISBN: 0-7364-1348-0
www.randomhouse.com/kids/disney

Printed in the United States of America   August 2002   10 9 8 7 6 5 4 3

One night in the dark castle of the evil Queen, a raven delivered a message from deep in the forest.

"Why, it's an invitation to the Duke's annual costume ball!" said the Queen. "And I, of course, will win first prize for the scariest costume of all."

The Queen sent for her royal
tailors and ordered them to make her
the scariest costume in all the land.
The tailors quickly went to work,
cutting and sewing the rarest silk.

"Try this one, Your Majesty," one tailor said to the Queen.

The evil Queen put her arms into the long sleeves of a shimmering black-and-silver costume with spindly spider legs sewn on.

"Wrong! All wrong!" the Queen shouted, looking at herself in the mirror. "Show me something else!"

"Perhaps a black bat?" the tailors asked. "Or maybe a slimy green monster for Her Majesty?"

But nothing pleased the Queen. "Do you want to lose your heads?" she shrieked. "Never mind! I'll do this myself!"

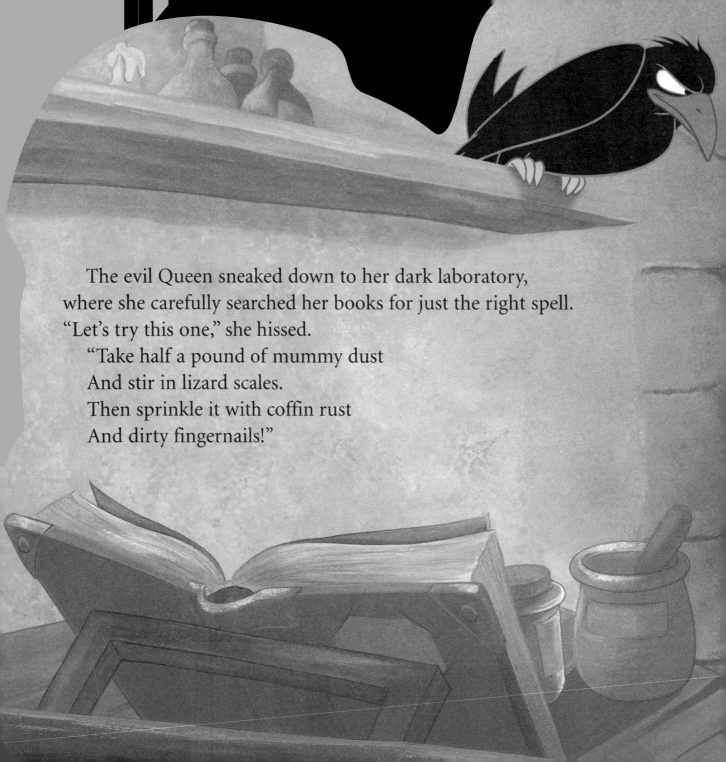

The evil Queen sneaked down to her dark laboratory,
where she carefully searched her books for just the right spell.
"Let's try this one," she hissed.
   "Take half a pound of mummy dust
   And stir in lizard scales.
   Then sprinkle it with coffin rust
   And dirty fingernails!"

Then the evil Queen held up the bubbling potion and, quick as a flash, drank it down!

"That's more like it," purred the evil Queen when she turned into a mean old hag. "Now all I have to do is ask the Magic Mirror to be sure."

"Magic Mirror on the wall,
Who is the scariest one of all?"
The Queen was shocked by the mirror's answer.
"My Queen, your costume is a fright,
But the scariest of all is the fair Snow White."

"What?" screamed the Queen. "That can't be!"

The Queen hurried down the stairs and found the sweet and lovely Snow White scrubbing the castle floors.

"The Mirror is surely mistaken!" exclaimed the evil Queen.
"No one will be scarier than I!"

That night, the Queen made her grand entrance at the ball, delighted with her scary costume.

"Why, it's monstrous, Your Majesty!" said a masked duchess.

"I'm sure it's the scariest costume I've ever seen!"
added the Duke.
"The Queen should win first prize!" everyone agreed.

The Queen was about to wrap
her bony fingers around the golden
trophy when the ballroom doors suddenly blew open. From out of the
night, a figure appeared—and a shadow fell over the entire room.
"Oh, my!" cried the Duke. "It's a . . . a . . . MONSTER!"

The creature moved closer.
"The castle is under attack!" cried the Duke.
"*WRAK!*" screeched the raven as everyone ran to hide.

But the Queen was not afraid.
"It is not a monster, you fools!" she
cried. "It's only a costume!"

"A costume?" asked the Duke, peeking out from under a table.
"It's magnificent!" the crowd said. "We've never seen one like it."

The Duke quickly took the
trophy and handed it to the magnificent
monster. "This costume takes
the prize!" he announced as the
party guests cheered.

And as the creature stopped
to thank the crowd . . .

. . . the Queen became furious!

There, under the mask, was the gentle face of Snow White! Using the scraps the Queen had left behind, Snow White had made her own scary costume.

"Horrid girl," the Queen muttered. "I should have locked her in the dungeon."

Snow White was truly the hit of the costume ball. The Queen was enraged, but would not let her anger show.

As the ball finally drew to an end, the Queen accepted the only prize she was going to win that night.

"And for Her Majesty, a blue ribbon for outstanding achievement in bobbing for apples!" the Duke announced. "Plus a bushel of apples from my private orchard!"

The Queen returned
to her throne room. "Whatever shall I
do with all these apples?" she wondered.
  "Oh, I'm sure I'll think of something,"
she said with a laugh—an evil laugh that sent
a chill through the entire kingdom.